Cooking

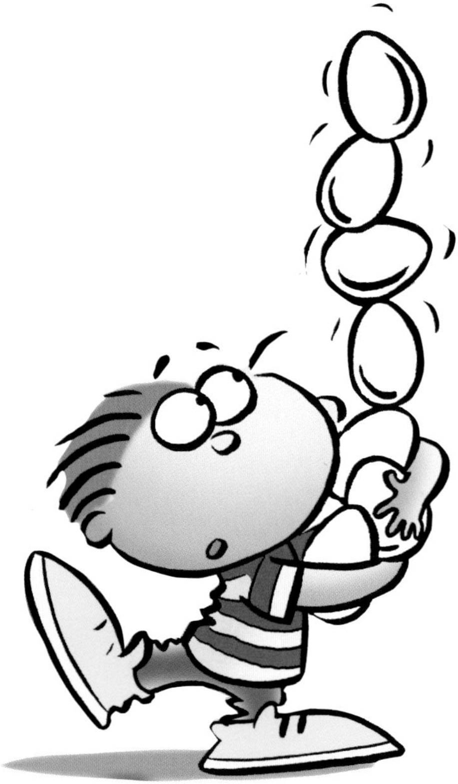

Illustrated by Brent Chambers

Rigby

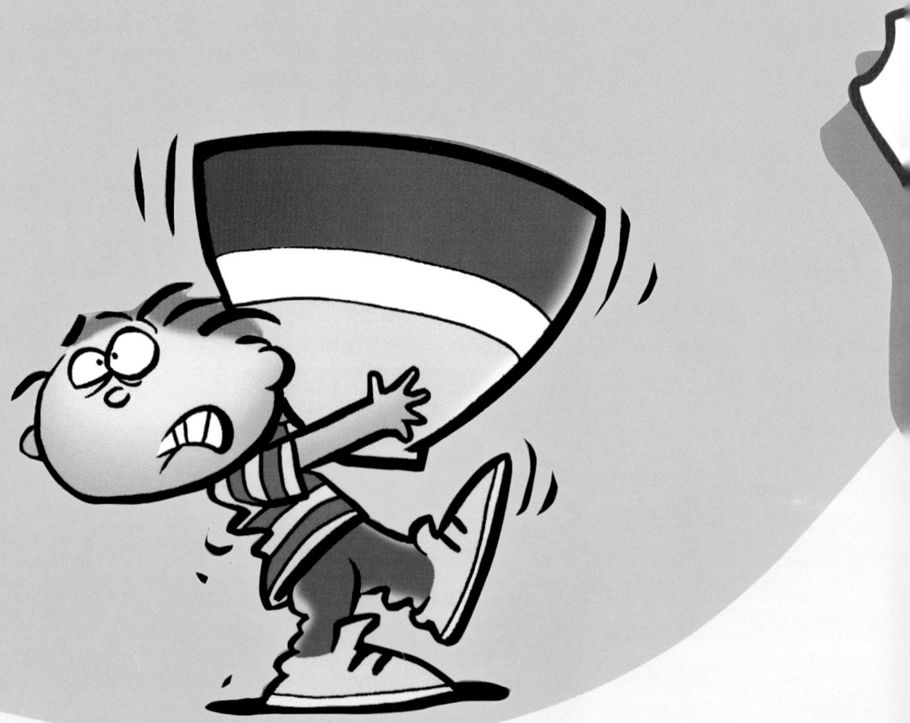

You can get
the bowl.

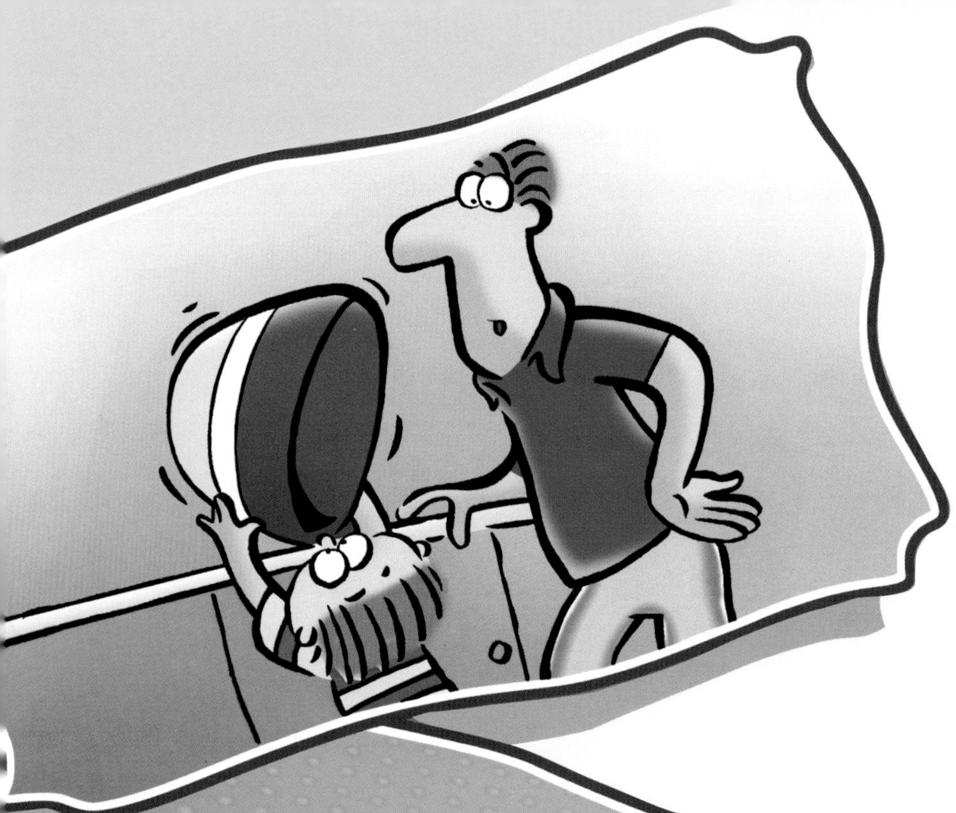

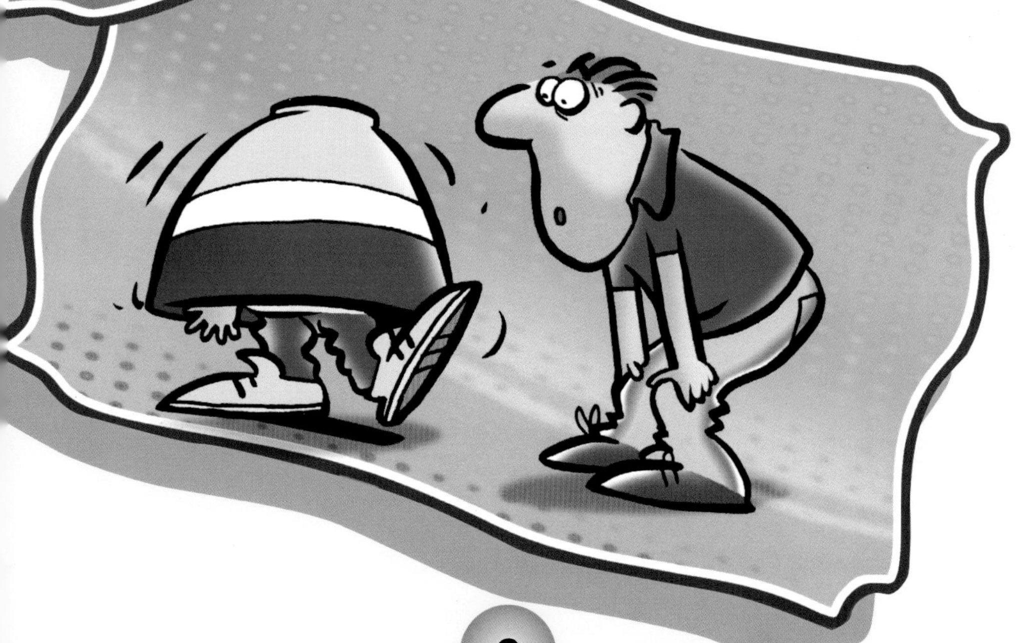

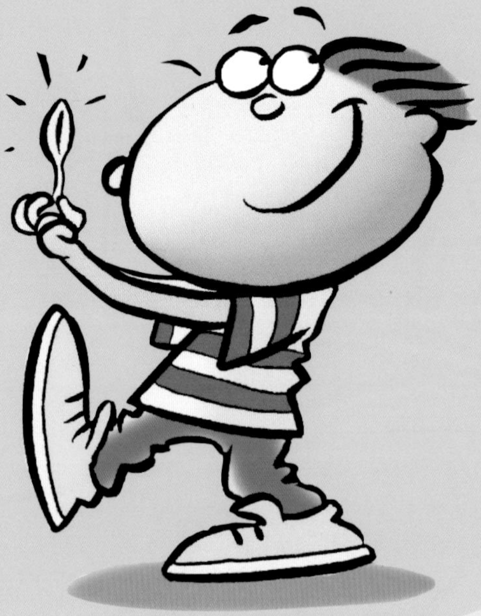

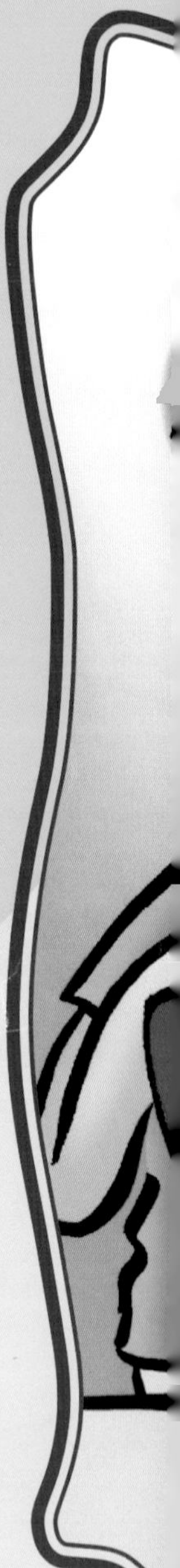

You can get
the spoon.

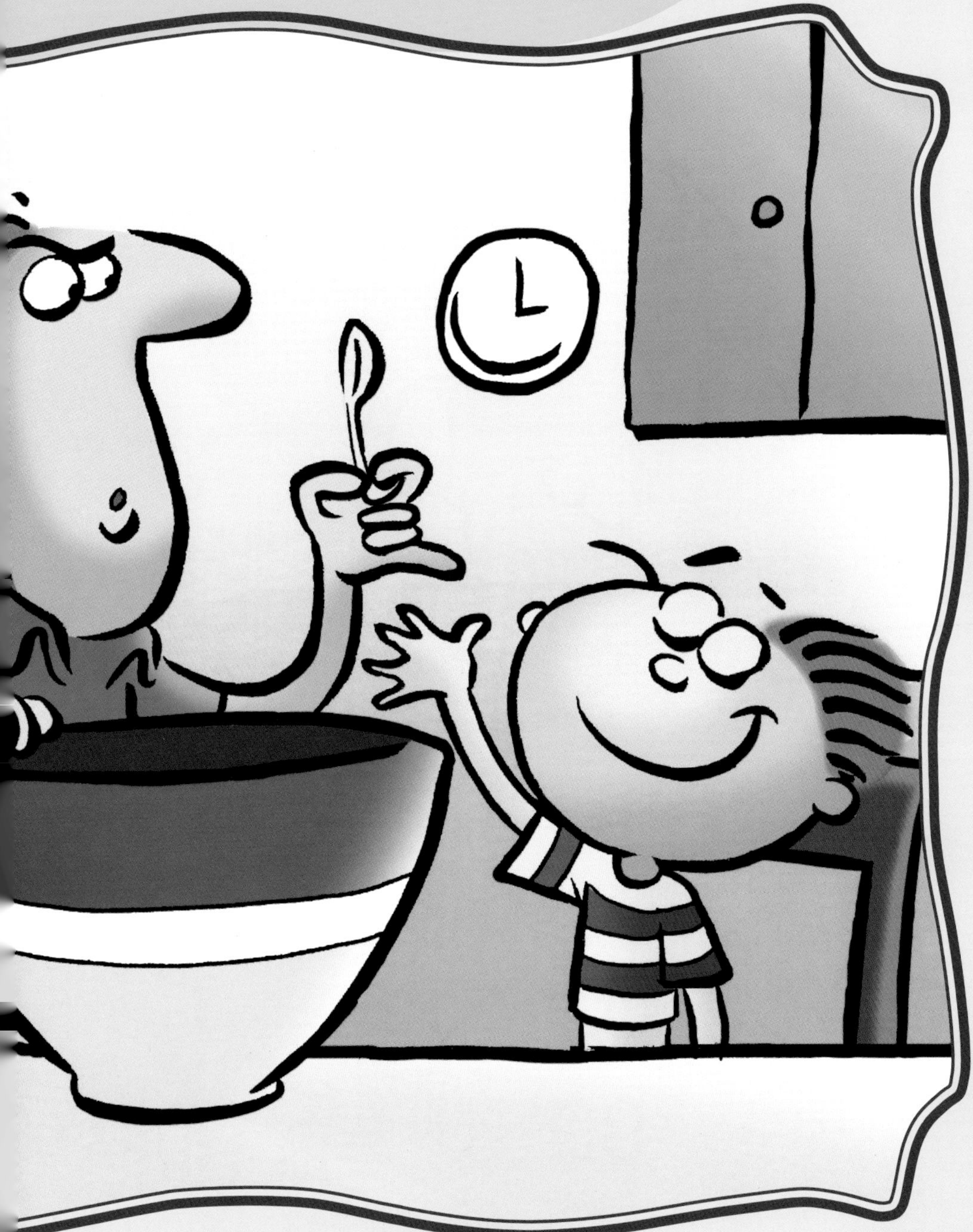

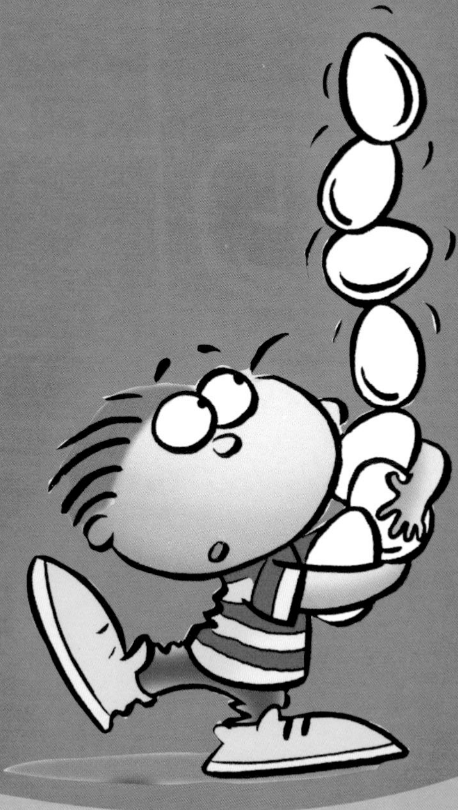

You can get
the eggs.

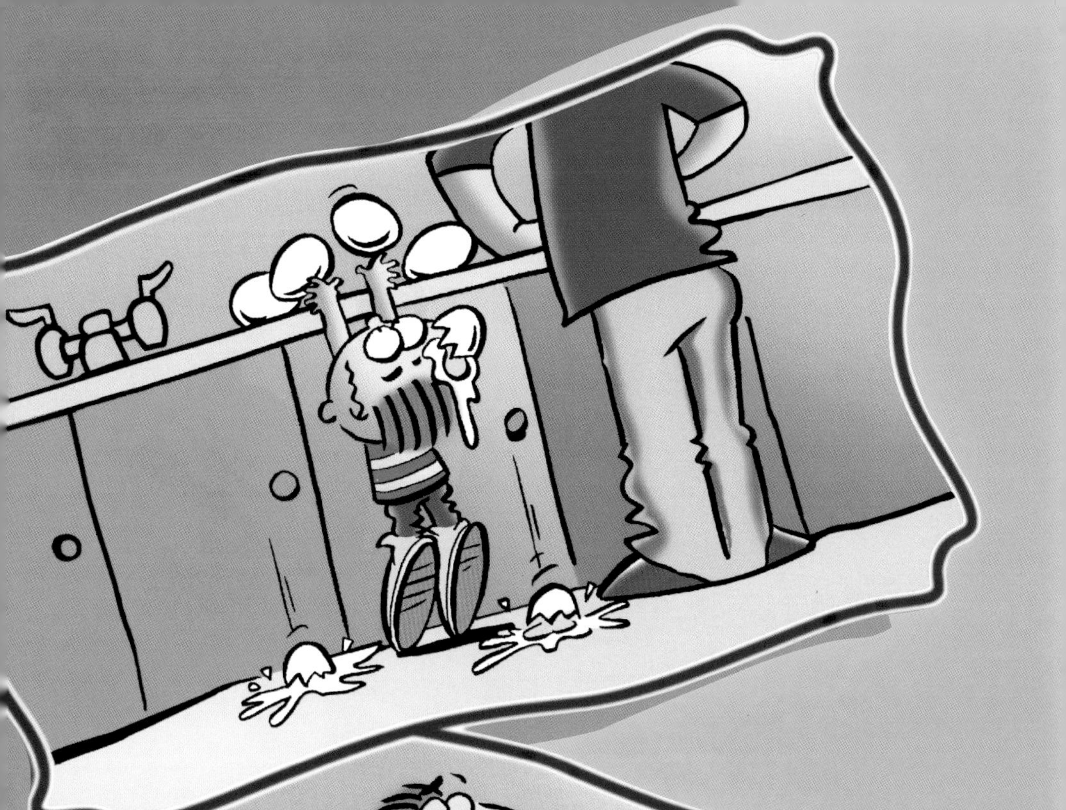

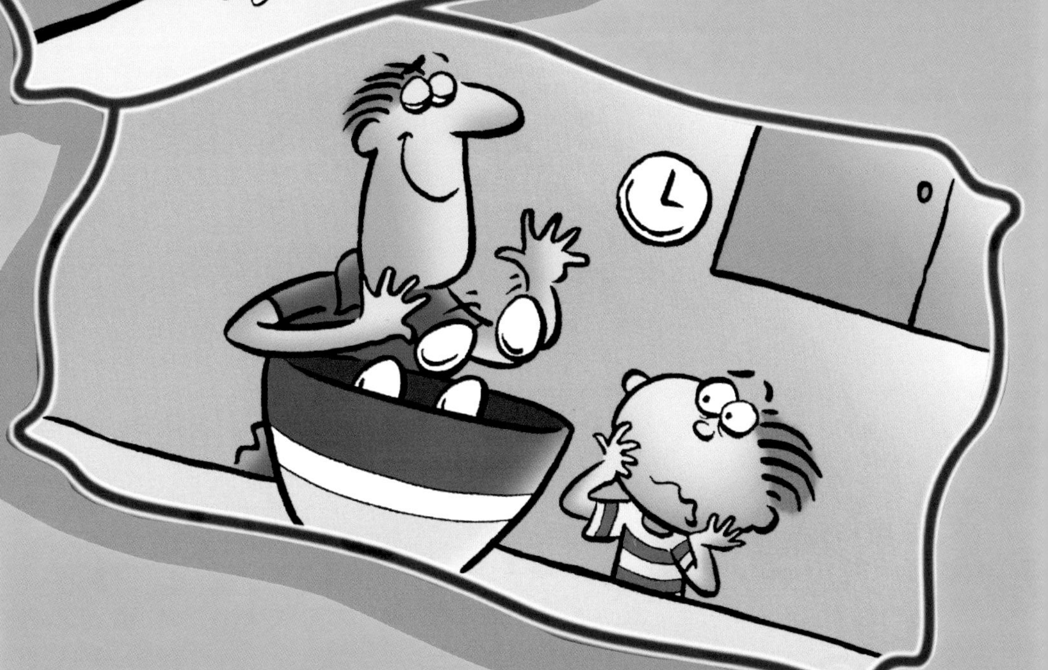

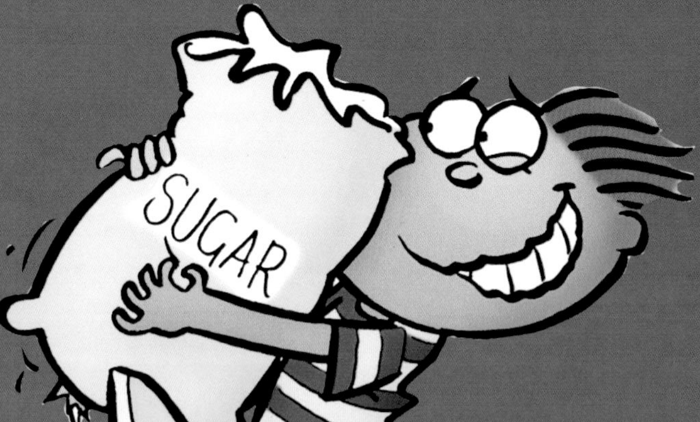

You can get
the sugar.

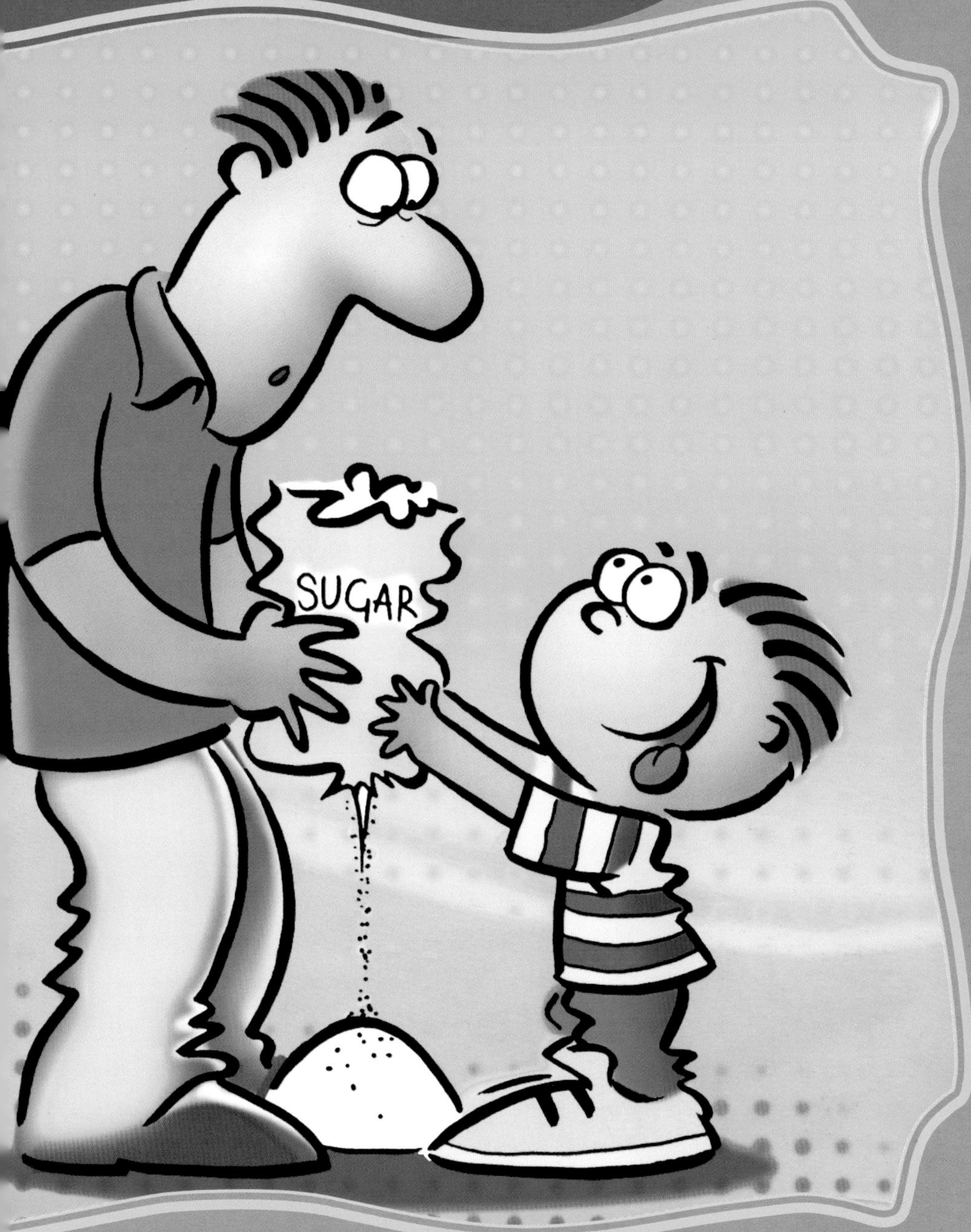
SUGAR

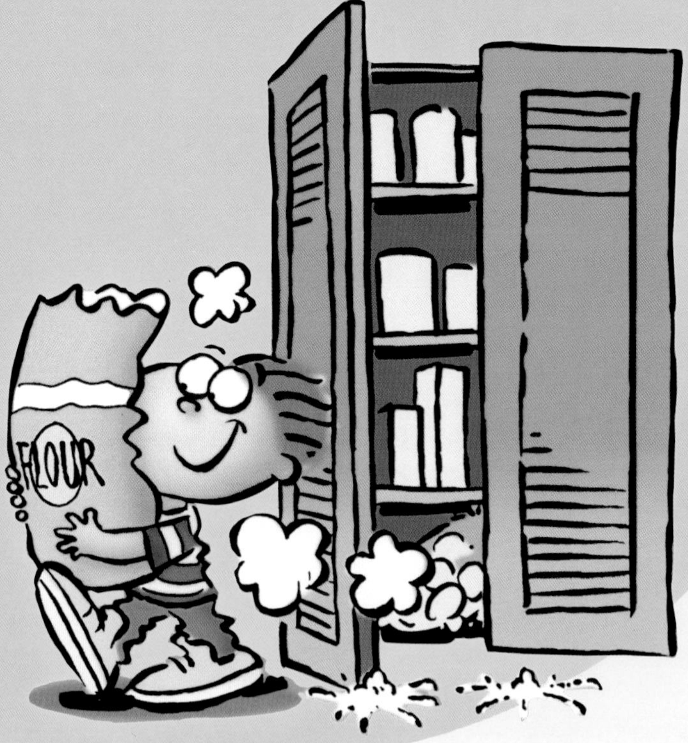

You can get the flour.

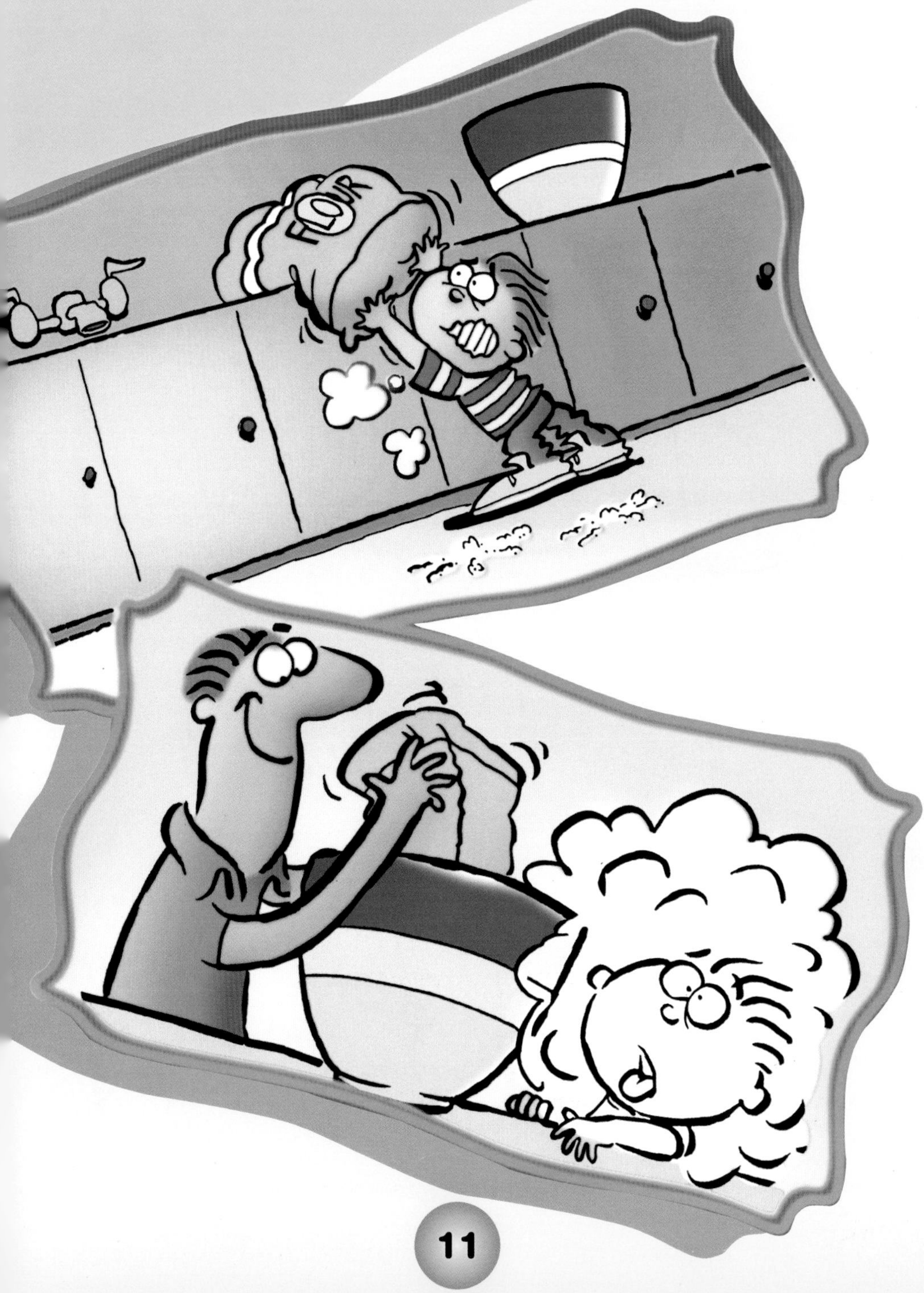
FLOUR

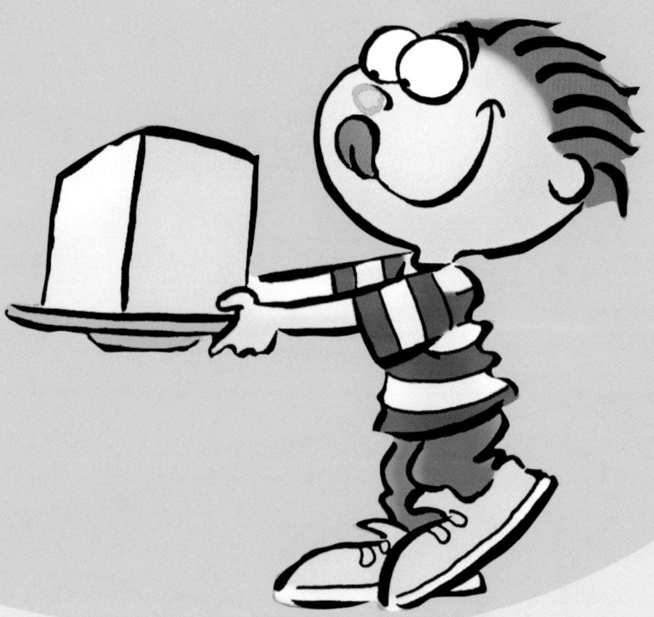

You can get
the butter.

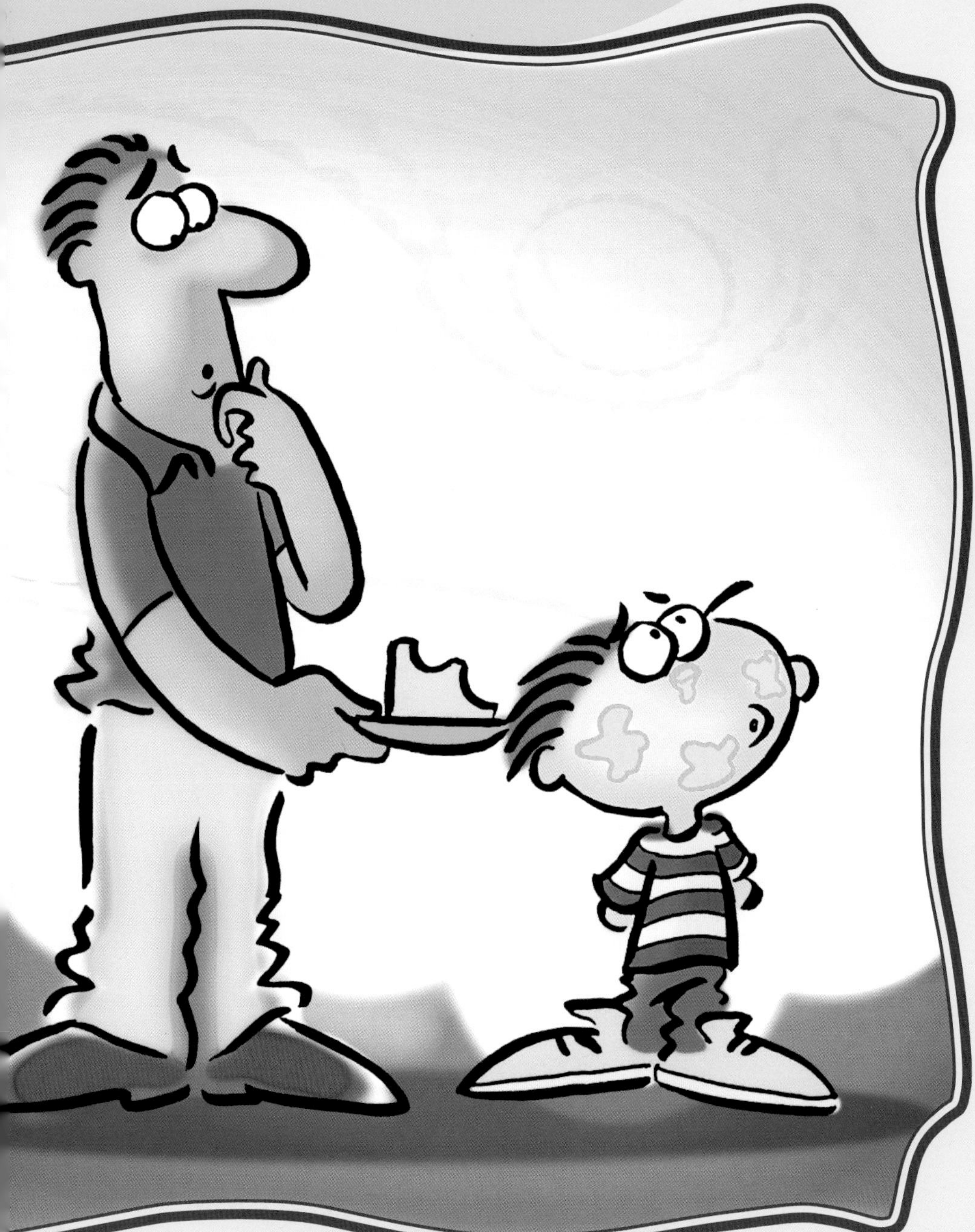

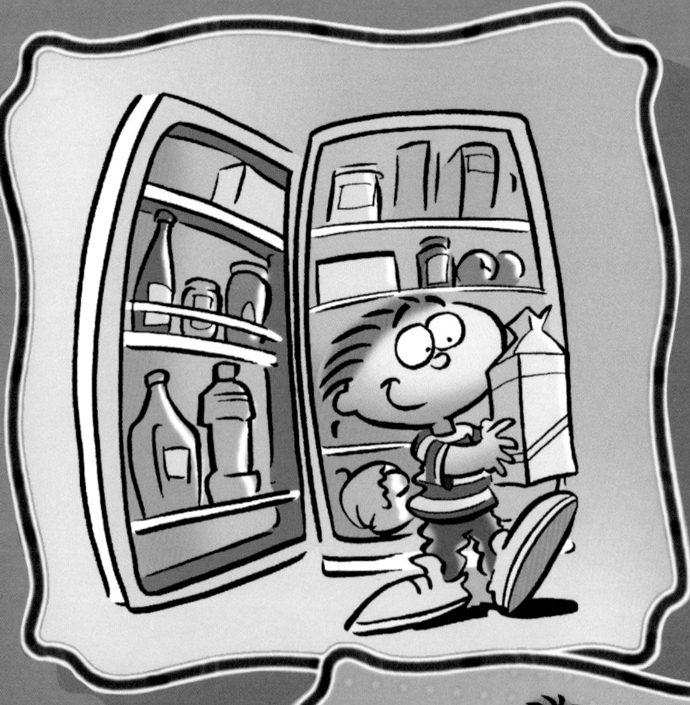

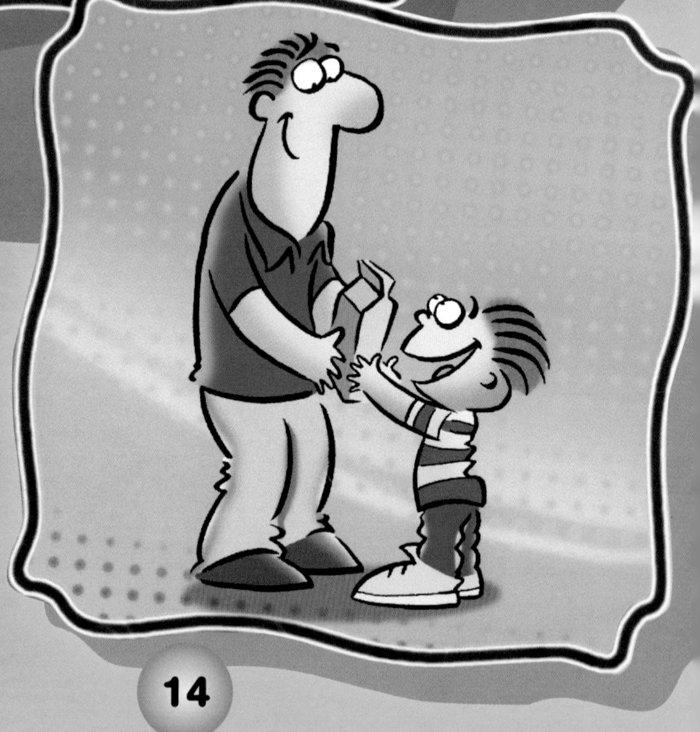

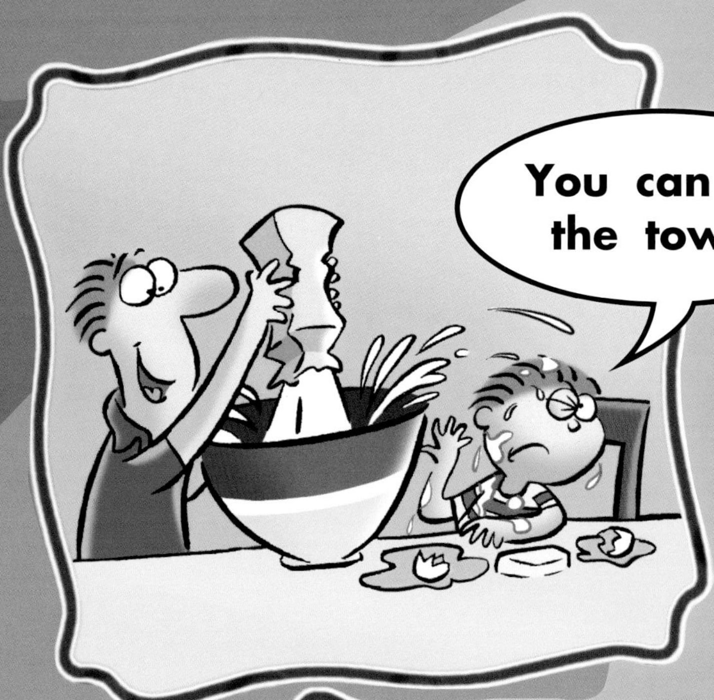
You can get
the towel.

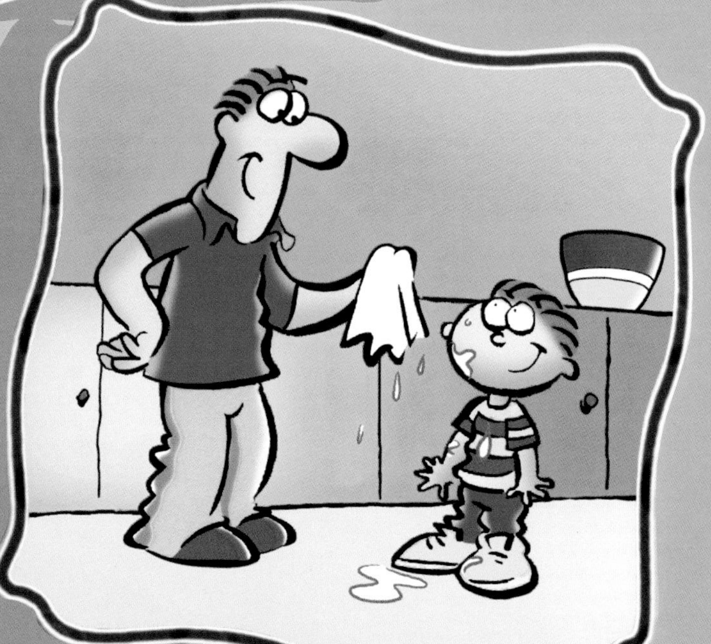

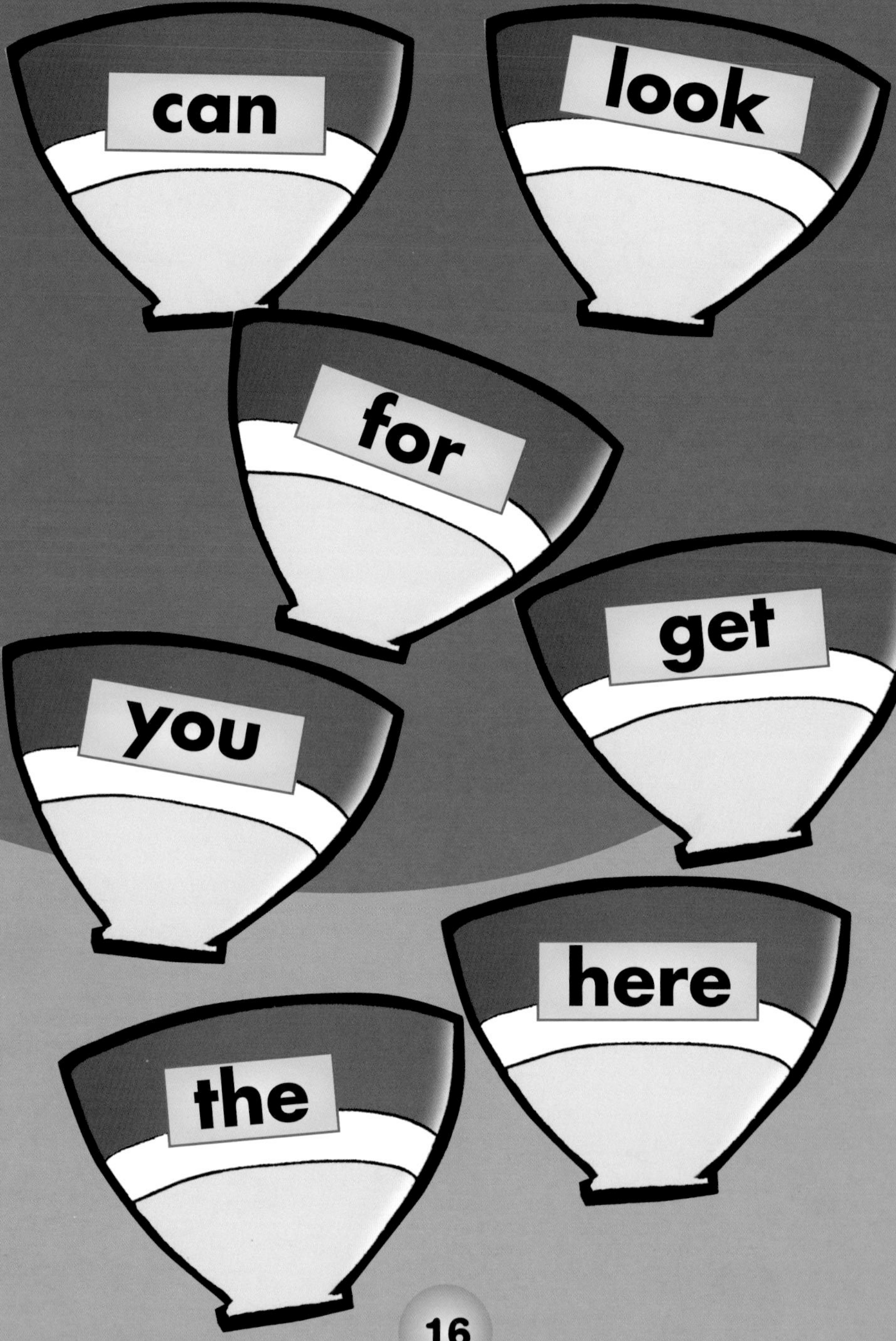
can
look
for
get
you
here
the